Sharing Books From Birth to Five

Welcome to Practical Parenting Books

It's never too early to introduce a child to books. It's wonderful to see your baby gazing intently at a cloth book; your toddler poring over a favourite picture; or your older child listening quietly to a story. And you're his favourite storyteller, so have fun together while you're reading – use silly voices, linger over the pictures and leave pauses for your child to join in.

As you read *Ten Sleepy Bunnies*, enjoy the guessing and the spotting activities as well as the first counting rhymes. First name all the different animals and make their sounds, then point out the numbers at the bottom of the page. Don't forget to count the smaller creatures as well as the big ones!

Books open doors to other worlds, so take a few minutes out of your busy day to cuddle up close and lose yourselves in a story. Your child will love it – and so will you.

Jane & Clare

Jane Kemp   Clare Walters

P.S. Look out, too, for *Tiny Trumpet*, the companion book in this age range, and all the other great books in the new Practical Parenting series.

AGE
2-3

First published in Great Britain
by HarperCollins Publishers Ltd in 2000

3 5 7 9 10 8 6 4 2
ISBN: 0-00-136171-6

The Practical Parenting/HarperCollins pre-school book series has been created by Jane Kemp and Clare Walters. The Practical Parenting imprimatur is used with permission by IPC Magazines Ltd.

Practical Parenting is published monthly by IPC Magazines Ltd. For subscription enquiries and orders, ring 01444 445555 or the credit card hotline (UK orders only) on 01622 778778.

The HarperCollins website address is: www.fireandwater.com

Manufactured in China

Ten Sleepy Bunnies

Written by Jane Kemp and Clare Walters

Illustrated by Peter Curry

Collins

An imprint of HarperCollinsPublishers

One busy mole
Digging underground,
Pops up her head
Guess who she's found?

1

one

Two woolly sheep
Munching on the grass,
In the sky above
Who's flying past?

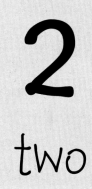

2
two

Three bright-eyed birds
Singing way up high,
On the branch below
Who scampers by?

3
three

Four cheeky squirrels
Clamber down the tree,
As they search for food
Who do they see?

4
four

Five dusty cows
Enjoy a long cool soak,
Down among the lilies
Can you hear a croak?

5
five

Croak croak

Six leaping frogs
Catch fat flies for tea,
Ripples on the water
Who can that be?

6
six

Seven sparkling fish
Shimmer as they swim,
Over by the bank
Who waddles in?

7

seven

Eight gliding ducks
Paddle in the reeds,
Which little animals
Are nibbling some seeds?

8
eight

Nine timid mice
Run beneath the gate,
Who's that hopping home
Now it's getting late?

9

nine

Squeak
squeak

Ten sleepy bunnies
Yawn beneath the moon,
Night night, sleep tight,
Morning will come soon.

10
ten

Sharing Books From Birth to Five

AGE 0-1

Zoo Patterns
A first focus cloth book
zebra runs
£3.99
0 00 136130 9

Teddy's Toys
A touch-and-feel cloth book
Teddy's Toys
£3.99
0 00 136132 5

AGE 1-2

Busy Babies Go Swimming
£3.99
0 00 136139 2

Busy Babies Go to the Gym
£3.99
0 00 136137 6

AGE 2-3

TINY TRUMPET
£3.99
0 00 136147 3

Ten Sleepy Bunnies
Learn to count from 1-10
£3.99
0 00 136171 6

AGE 3-5

Rocket to the Rescue
Meet Jessie and Joe of Little Oak Farm
£3.99
0 00 136151 1

The Piggy Race
Meet Jessie and Joe of Little Oak Farm
£3.99
0 00 136153 8

The Practical Parenting books are available from all good bookshops and can be ordered direct from HarperCollins Publishers by ringing 0141 7723200 and through the HarperCollins website: www.fireandwater.com

You can also order any of these titles, with free post and packaging, from the Practical Parenting Bookshop on 01326 569339 or send your cheque or postal order together with your name and address to: Practical Parenting Bookshop, Freepost, PO Box 11, Falmouth, TR10 9EN.